for Siggy and all my young friends

John Speirs'
Margaret Wise Brown
Treasury
14 Classic Stories and Poems

A Gold Key Book
Western Publishing Company, Inc.

CONTENTS

The Children's Year

SPRING

The wind blows strong across the hill
And slaps the yellow daffodil,
The red feathery trees
And the sharp green leaves
Remind the farmer to plant his seeds
In the brown earth where the old roots stir,
And early in the morning
The small birds sing.

SUMMER

Now in July
To lie in the sweet grass
With the earth so near
That you can hear
The murmur of insects,
Summer sound,
And almost hear the earth turn round
While far away in the still blue sky
A sudden storm goes rumbling by.

AUTUMN

Apples heavy and red
Bend the branches down,
Grapes are purple
And nuts are brown,
The apples smell sharp and sweet on the ground
Where the yellow bees go buzzing around.
And way up high
The birds fly southward
Down the sky.

WINTER

December comes;
The white snow comes again;
It falls softly in the night
White
From the dark blue sky.
It covers the earth that the spring kept green
And summer kept warm.
It covers the earth where the autumn leaves fell
Golden on the ground.
All is white.
All is still.
And Christmas trees shine green as emeralds
With rubies and diamonds and sapphires
On Christmas night.

The Little Toy Train

In the little green house lived a cat and a mouse,
 a girl and a boy,
  and a man with a little toy train.
One day the train ran away.
 It was a very little train.
  So it ran down a mouse hole.
   And the cat and the mouse
    and the girl and the boy
     and the man who were all very little too
      ran down the mouse hole after
       the little toy train.

And the little toy train ran far away following rabbit
tracks in the grass until it popped down a rabbit's hole
and woke up seventeen little rabbits who went right
back to sleep again until
     the cat
      and the mouse
       and the girl
        and the boy
         and the man
          came running after the little toy train
           and woke all seventeen little rabbits
            up again.

And so the seventeen little rabbits
   ran after the little toy train
And the little toy train ran on and away
   through a field of clover and timothy hay,
    through a hole in a tree
     and a hole in a stone
      and a hole in the air
       near a telephone pole,

through a log
and a pond
near a big green frog,
   through a keyhole into a baker's shop
and on
   and on
    without a stop
followed by seventeen rabbits
   a man
    a boy
     a girl
      a cat
       and a mouse
Until it came to the little green house and
   ran home again,
And that was the trip of the little toy train.

Said a Fish to a Fish

Said a fish to a fish,
　"Look away up high.
　　What is that shadow
　　　Under the sky?
　　　　That great dark shadow sailing by,
　　　Over the ocean,
　　　Under the sky."

Said a fish to a fish,
"That shadow up high
Is a yellow fish
With a yellow eye
That goes swimming along
Under the sky."

"Come, little fish,
　Let us fly fly fly
　Up where that shadow is
　Under the sky."

So up they swam,
Away up high

Where they could see
With their fishes' eye
The great dark shadow sailing by,
The slow dark shadow
Under the sky.

But the slow dark shadow
Under the sky
Was no yellow fish
With a yellow eye.
For they could see
With their fishes' eye
That the slow dark shadow
Under the sky
Was a fishing boat
Sailing,
Sailing by
Over the ocean
Under the sky.

"Come, little fishes,
Fly fly fly,
Fly from that fishing boat
Under the sky,
Come down in the ocean
Away from the sky."

And the fishing boat sailed by.

Wind in the Corn

I heard the wind in the corn one day,
I knew that it came from far away,
And it rustled the trembling corn to say
That it was going far away
And could not stay,
Could never stay.

Count to Ten

(With Thanks to Lear)

1

There was once a little owl
Count to one
1
one little owl

2

There were two little trolls
 roly
  poly
Count to two
1, 2
two little trolls

3

There were three little pigs
 piggy
  wiggy
   dance a jiggy
Count to three
1, 2, 3
three little pigs

4

There were four little foxes
  clocksy
   foxy
    doxy
     hide behind the rocks
Count to four
1, 2, 3, 4
four little foxes

5

There were five little fish
  fishy
   squishy
    slishy
     in a dishy
      very swishy
Count to five
1, 2, 3, 4, 5
five little fish

6

Six little pickles
  tickle
   trickle
    sickle
     fickle
      stickle
       crickle
Count to six
1, 2, 3, 4, 5, 6
six little pickles

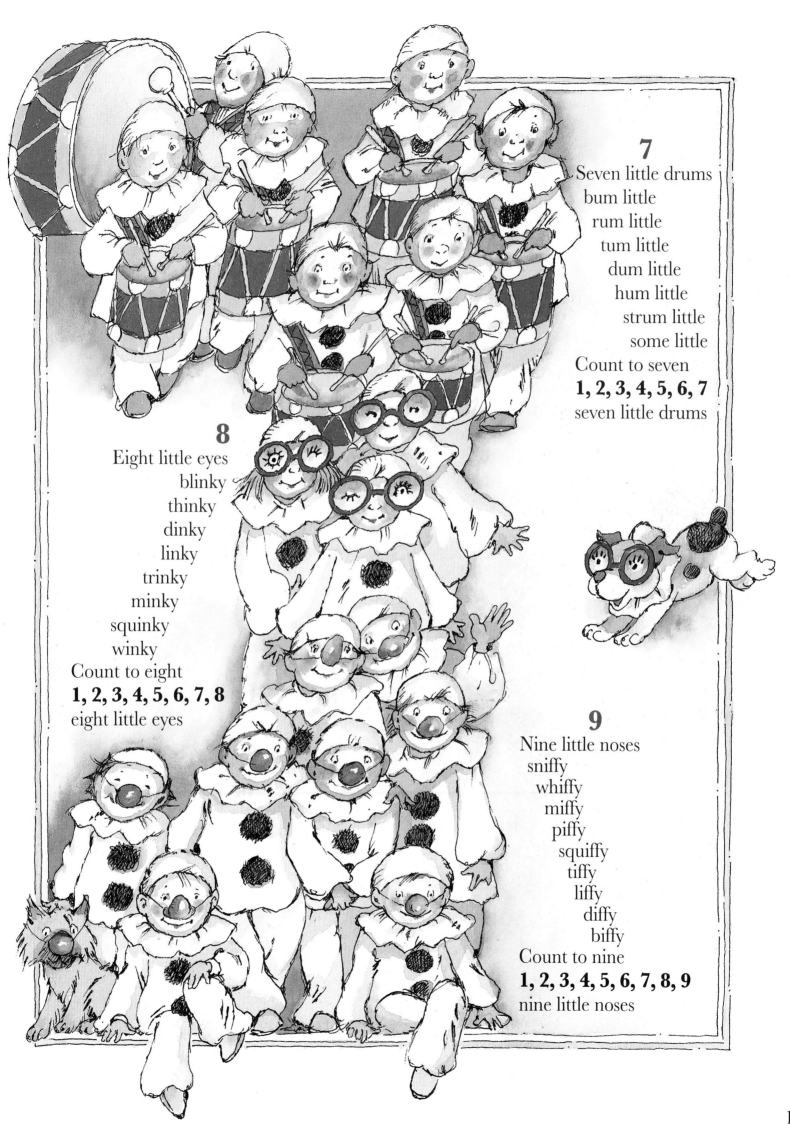

7

Seven little drums
bum little
rum little
tum little
dum little
hum little
strum little
some little
Count to seven
1, 2, 3, 4, 5, 6, 7
seven little drums

8

Eight little eyes
blinky
thinky
dinky
linky
trinky
minky
squinky
winky
Count to eight
1, 2, 3, 4, 5, 6, 7, 8
eight little eyes

9

Nine little noses
sniffy
whiffy
miffy
piffy
squiffy
tiffy
liffy
diffy
biffy
Count to nine
1, 2, 3, 4, 5, 6, 7, 8, 9
nine little noses

10
Ten little kings
  kingy
   ringy
    singy
     dingy
      lingy
       stringy
        flingy
         mingy
          quick and clingy
           wild and wingy
Count to ten
1, 2, 3, 4, 5, 6, 7, 8, 9, 10
ten little kings

The Bluefish

A fisherman went fishing,
Went fishing for a fish.
He went fishing for the bluefish
That swims down below.
Jerk Jerk Jerk
Went the fisherman's line,
Pull Pull Pull
His line pulled so.

Ho Ho Ho
Can this be the bluefish
That swims down below?

He pulled in the fish
On the hook on his line
And he looked at the fish
On the hook on his line,
Then the fisherman said,

No
This is just a yellow fish
And I will let him go
So
He let the fish go.

Then the fisherman went fishing
For another fish,
He went fishing for the bluefish
That swims down below.

He caught red fish and green fish
And fast fish and slow,
But he never caught the bluefish
That swims down below.

19

The Wild Garden

In this garden you will find
No columbine or eglantine.
All the flowers that you will find
Were found by me and they are mine.
You will find white violets from the woods
That I dug up in the spring,
And you will find daisies from the fields,
And one buttercup.
I planted lots of buttercup seeds
But only one came up.

Here come the bees with a great big buzz,
Yellow and black and covered with fuzz.

Here come the flies in a big black swarm
To tickle a fat little girl's bare arm.

Here come the beetles all shiny and green
And red and yellow and shiny and mean
to leaves and roots.

Here comes a butterfly first to fly
Out of June and into July.

And here sleeps a
   sleepy young firefly.

Every spring they come again,
Yellow flowers in the rain,
And lambs are born
And birds are born
In the soft green early morn.

The red bird whistles in the tree.
Spring is here
Endlessly
Ceaselessly
For an instant
In a tree.

Wild strawberries
Are wild,
They taste wild
And their roots run wild
Through the ground,
And they hide like
Little wild red strawberries
In the grass,
And you see them
Suddenly
Small and red
And wild.

Eyes in the Night

The moon came up on a summer's night
That was soft and dark except for the light
Of fireflies and the gleaming eyes
Of green-eyed cats and the amber eyes of wandering dogs
And the red eyes of frogs and the eye of the toad
Picked up by lights coming down the road,
Little emerald eyes, the gleaming eyes,
And the eyes of rabbits and foxes
And more and more flickering fireflies.
Then the car went by, and soon
There was only the light
Of a big warm moon
All over the summer night.

The Boy Who Belonged to the Cat

Once there was a little boy and he belonged to a cat and was brought up by a cat and he was the healthiest, happiest little boy in the world.

Instead of opening his eyes slowly in the morning, he blinked them open. So did the cat.

And then they began to stretch and to yawn. The cat shot out one leg and spread the pads of her paws. So the boy shot one foot forward in bed and spread his toes. He spread his fingers. Then he shot out his other leg and stretched his toes and at the same time on the end of his arms he stretched all his fingers out like cat paws or starfish and yawned again. Then he stretched his little stomach and back and got up.

And while the cat washed her eyes and her whiskers with her tongue and her paw, he washed with a big wet washrag.

Then they went out and sat and dried themselves in the warm sun and blinked at the world and thought their first thoughts without a word. And the sun shone on them and warmed their bones.

Then they were hungry and they both drank their milk.

And some mornings they would have a little fish.

At noon the cat gave the little boy green vegetables because he didn't like green grass and the cat didn't really care whether she ate hot green string beans or cold green grass. But the boy did.

Then after lunch the cat found a quiet place, curled in a warm ball, purred a little, and fell asleep. All day long whenever the cat or the boy had nothing to do or had done too much, they would take these little catnaps—why not?

All the better to grow on, purred the cat.

So the cat taught the little boy to watch quietly and to sit in the sun and to keep out of big smells and big noises and big crowds. And he was the happiest, healthiest little boy in the world and very glad that he belonged to a cat.

The Little Flat Flounder

Once there was a little flat flounder with two eyes on the top of his head who lived in the depths of the sea.

Around was green water and under the water was sand and seaweed and a few dark rocks where the blue-black lobsters crawled, slowly opening and shutting their claws.

From their long stalked beady black lobster eyes they looked into the cold blue eyes of the flounder and the dark gray-blue eyes of the cod and the pollack and haddock, and into the brown-black eyes of the skate, and into the yellow eyes of the mackerel.

Fish never close their eyes.

Even when they sleep, fish never close their eyes.

So there lay the little flounder flat in the sand with his gray-blue eyes wide open, night and day.

He watched for food and he watched for danger.

And the minute the flounder saw the lobster he hid in the soft wet sand.

For the lobster with the snapping claws was no friend of the flounder.

The little flounder had plenty of enemies waiting to dive through the sea to catch him.

It seemed as though everything in the air and in the water was after the little flounder.

They were all after the little flounder.

The fish hawk was after him, ready to plunge down on him, down through the water like a rock from the sky.

If he didn't keep well hidden in the sand at low tide, the blue heron was there waiting to dip his long neck down for him.

Or the gulls were swooping to dive for him.

And always the fish hawk would hover, waiting, his two striped wings spread across the air, his sharp bird eye peering down through the waters for the moving shadow that would be a fish. And, of course, he hoped that the fish would be a flounder—a little flat flounder.

But it was not only the hawks and the herons and the gulls that were after the flounder.

The other fish were after him, too—the codfish, the dogfish, the skate. The mackerel, the halibut, and the shad.

And the only way for him to escape from them was to hide.

The little flat flounder could make himself so much like the sand and seaweed he lay on that no one could see he was there. Wherever the little flounder humped himself, his coloring changed with the parts of the sea. He was a chameleon of the ocean deep.

The fishermen were after him, too, with hooks and lines and nets, but he stuck to the clams and sea fleas and sandworms on the bottom of the sea for his food.

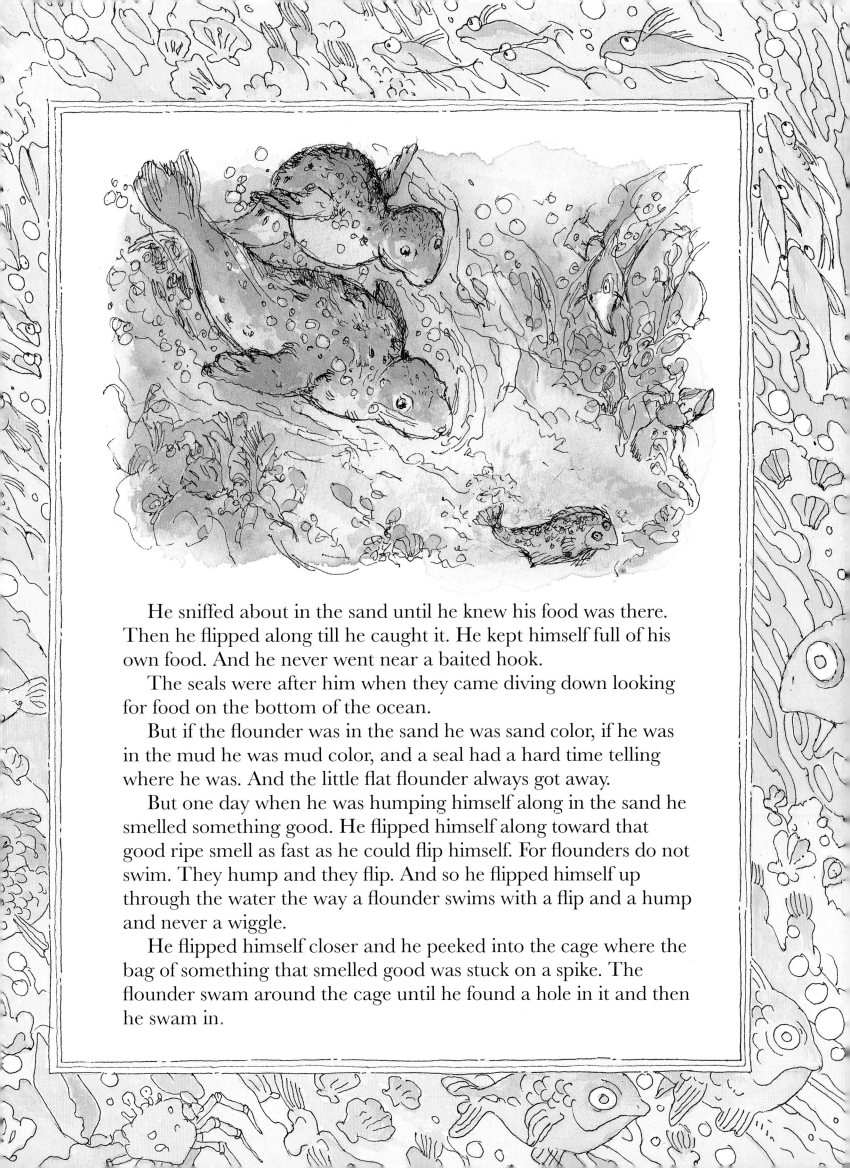

He sniffed about in the sand until he knew his food was there. Then he flipped along till he caught it. He kept himself full of his own food. And he never went near a baited hook.

The seals were after him when they came diving down looking for food on the bottom of the ocean.

But if the flounder was in the sand he was sand color, if he was in the mud he was mud color, and a seal had a hard time telling where he was. And the little flat flounder always got away.

But one day when he was humping himself along in the sand he smelled something good. He flipped himself along toward that good ripe smell as fast as he could flip himself. For flounders do not swim. They hump and they flip. And so he flipped himself up through the water the way a flounder swims with a flip and a hump and never a wiggle.

He flipped himself closer and he peeked into the cage where the bag of something that smelled good was stuck on a spike. The flounder swam around the cage until he found a hole in it and then he swam in.

Inside the cage he flipped himself among the crabs and sea urchins and lobsters and took a big bite of the bait. And another bite of the bait. For that was what that good smell was—herring bait, in a lobster pot.

But when he tried to get out of the cage he was trapped. Trapped in a lobster pot!

Poor little flounder, what would he do now? He turned a funny green and black color so that you could scarcely see him there at the bottom of the lobster pot.

But still he couldn't get out.

Night came on and darkened the sea.

Day came on and brightened the sea and the warmth of the sun came down through the green water.

And then there was a pull, a jerk, and there was the lobster pot moving up through the waters toward the sun.

Right out into the air it came. And over the sides of the lobsterman's boat it was hauled. The lobsterman reached in and pulled out the lobsters, pegged their claws so they couldn't bite, and dropped them in the bottom of his boat.

He brushed out the green prickly sea urchins and dropped them back in the sea. He pulled out the sea cucumbers and the conch shells and the sea spiders, and threw them all back into the sea, where they sank slowly down till they disappeared in the water.

Last of all, he pulled out the flounder.

"A fine fried flounder I'll make of you," said the lobsterman. "Though you are too little for dinner and too small for lunch you will make a fine little tidbit for breakfast."

And he laid the little flat flounder carefully on the gunnel of his boat.

A tidbit for breakfast indeed! The lobsterman did not realize what a smart, strong little flat flounder he had caught. For with a flip and a hump the little flounder flipped himself into the air and overboard into the sea—just like that.

And night came on again in the sea.

And the lobsterman went home with his lobsters.

And all the sea gulls went home to their sea gull nests.

And the fish hawks to their fish hawk nests.

And the blue heron to where the blue heron goes.

And the fish swam sleepily about in the darkened sea.

And the flounder dozed on the bottom, with his eyes still open.

The Seven Weathers

One day a little dog had to stay indoors because
he hated to get his feet wet and that was the day it rained

and it snowed   and the fog rolled in   and there was a tornado

and a hurricane   and a breeze   and a shower.

Then the sun came out and all the flowers came up because
it was spring and then the sun shone and the little dog went out
to take a walk before nightfall on his four soft feet, just in time—

Because then the stars came out and it was night
and the wind began to blow all sorts of lovely evening
smells to his nose.

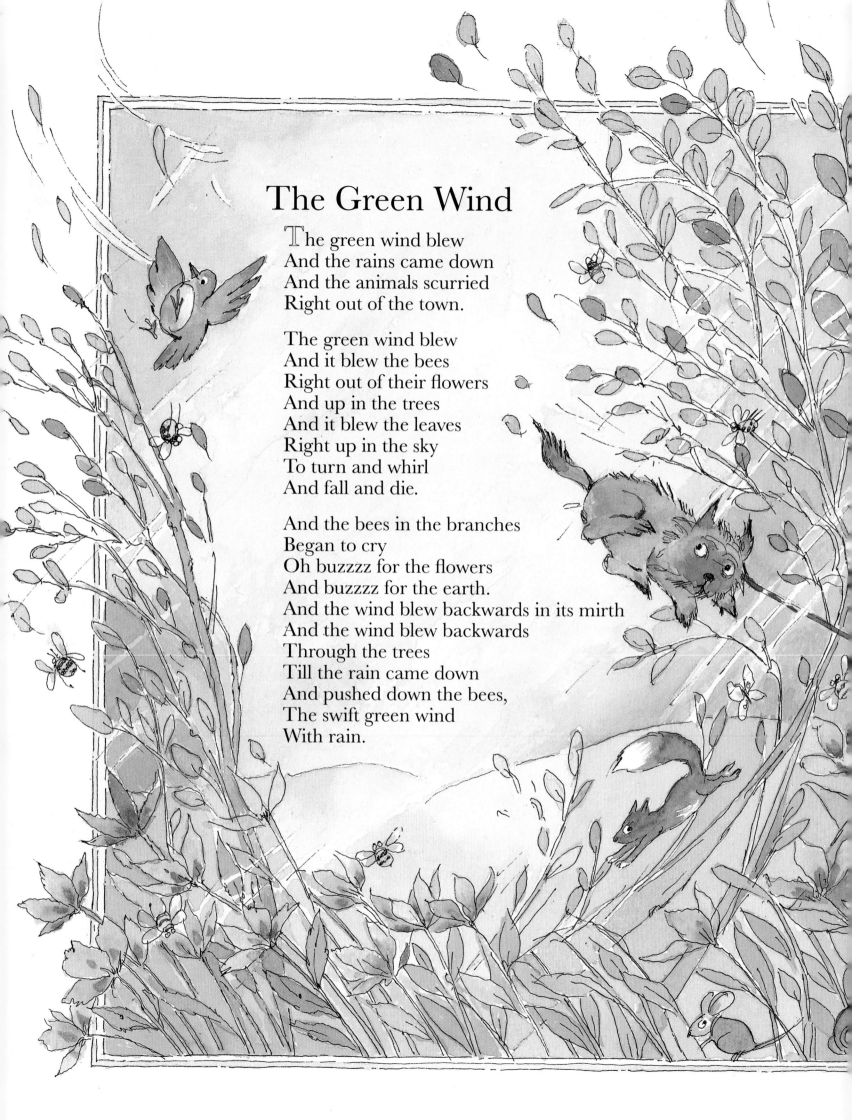

The Green Wind

The green wind blew
And the rains came down
And the animals scurried
Right out of the town.

The green wind blew
And it blew the bees
Right out of their flowers
And up in the trees
And it blew the leaves
Right up in the sky
To turn and whirl
And fall and die.

And the bees in the branches
Began to cry
Oh buzzzz for the flowers
And buzzzz for the earth.
And the wind blew backwards in its mirth
And the wind blew backwards
Through the trees
Till the rain came down
And pushed down the bees,
The swift green wind
With rain.

The Wonderful Room

There was a wonderful room with a big red bed and a vast gray rug with soldiers and drums on it and a glass fireplace and a big fur chair and a little table with a cake on it and a book with nothing in it and a book with something in it and an ocean outside the window with seven boats sailing on it and a picture on the wall of a horse with a hat on his head and a picture of a panda kicking a panda

and a wooden soldier

and a golden hunting horn

and by the fire in the glass fireplace sat a cat and a dog and a sleepy old owl who lived in this wonderful room and a hole in the wall where a little mouse lived and nobody knew he was there.

And there was a great big hump under the white sheets on the big red bed and who could that be hiding there with one bare foot wiggling its toes sticking out from under the covers?

And over the bed was a light like a star and on the ceiling were starfish that stayed there because they were glued onto the ceiling. And in four little vases were wild flowers and wild flowers and wild flowers, and wild flowers picked from a field at noon— buttercups, clovers, and daisies. And there were wild violets from the woods

and wild geraniums

and wild strawberry blossoms

and yellow star flowers

and blue star flowers

and dogtooth violets

and white violets

and one jack-in-the-pulpit

and another buttercup

and three kinds of clover.

So Many Nights

So many nights.
Blue nights,
Brown nights,
And the sudden lights
In deep black nights
Of stars
And cars
And airplanes
And soft gray nights when it rains
And blue nights with a foggy moon
Smoking in the trees

And pink and red nights
Above great cities
And silver nights all filled with stars
And misty nights when a white mist
Drifts
And lifts over the white-topped fields
And purple nights beyond the lights
Of your own room
And blue snowy nights
And night that is just
Dark bright night.